W9-DBE-136

Milk

The Big Bunny and the Magic Show

by Steven Kroll
illustrated by Janet Stevens

SCHOLASTIC INC.
New York Toronto London Auckland Sydney

For JOHN and KATE BRIGGS,
who make everything magical

ISBN 0-590-44633-9

This edition published by Scholastic Inc., 730 Broadway, New York, NY 10003, by arrangement with Holiday House, Inc.

12 11 10 9 8 7 6 5 4 5/9

Printed in the U.S.A. 08

First Scholastic printing, March 1987

It was a few days before Easter. Wilbur, the great big Easter Bunny, had finished his work early. He'd woven new wicker baskets and dyed all the Easter eggs. He'd painted designs on the eggs and made oodles of jelly beans and chocolate candy. All he had to do now was deliver everything.

Last year Wilbur had gotten sick on Easter Eve. He'd almost missed his deliveries. This year he was fine but grumpy. And when he woke up and looked out on those big piles of Easter goodies, he said, "Hmph, I'm tired of being the Easter Bunny."

He pulled on his bathrobe and thumped into the kitchen to have breakfast. There wasn't much in the fridge. He had two big carrots and a cup of tea. As he was finishing, he picked up *The Daily Bunny Bulletin.*

There, on page two, was an ad: MAGICIAN NEEDS BUNNY! FOR TRICKS AND TRAVEL. INTERVIEWS, TOWN SQUARE, TODAY. The ad was signed *Morgan the Magician.*

Just then there was a knock on Wilbur's door. In tumbled his four bunny friends.

"We came to see if you were ready for Easter," said Hector and Francine.

"We're sure glad you're not sick this year," said Charles and Henrietta.

"Have you seen this ad?" asked Wilbur.

The four bunnies stared at the newspaper.

"I've decided to get a new job," said Wilbur.

"But Easter is only a few days away!" cried Hector.

"You can't look for another job now," said Charles.

"Oh, yes I can!" said Wilbur. And he dashed out the door.

The bunnies looked at one another.

"We've got to stop him!" said Henrietta.

They all rushed after Wilbur.

When they reached the town square, hundreds of bunnies were lined up outside an old truck. MORGAN'S MAGIC SHOW was painted on the side in bright letters.

Wilbur was nowhere to be seen.

The four bunnies raced up to the truck and peered through the side window. Morgan the Magician was twirling the ends of his mustache. He was talking to Wilbur.

"Why do you want this job?" he asked.

"I'm sick of what I'm doing now," said Wilbur.

"What's that?" asked Morgan.

"I'm the Easter Bunny."

Morgan burst out laughing. "But everyone knows you're not supposed to *see* the Easter Bunny."

"That's one of the reasons I want to quit. I'm tired of hiding," said Wilbur.

Morgan's eyes sparkled like diamonds. "I think you'll make a fine assistant," he said. "You're hired."

The four bunnies clapped their paws to their heads.

"Oh, no!" said Hector.

"Who's going to deliver the eggs?" wailed Francine.

"Wilbur knows we're too small to carry all of them," said Charles.

"We've got to make him change his mind," said Henrietta.

Morgan the Magician hung a sign outside the truck. BUNNY HIRED, it said. Then he jumped behind the wheel and drove off in a cloud of dust.

The bunnies choked and sneezed.

"Quick!" said Hector. "After them!"

The four bunnies ran and got their bicycle built for four. They pedaled off down the road after the truck. They pedaled and pedaled.

"I've got an idea for getting Wilbur back," said Henrietta.

She quickly told it to the three other bunnies.

"Great!" said Hector.

"I think Wilbur will quit after this," said Francine.

"It's worth a try," said Charles.

"There's a theater in the next town," said Francine.

"I bet Wilbur and Morgan will be there," said Charles.

When the bunnies arrived in the next town, they saw Morgan's truck parked in front of the theater. The magic show was just about to begin. The bunnies sneaked into the theater through the back door. Morgan the Magician was getting ready to go onstage. Wilbur stood beside him, wearing a long, ruffled cape and a wig.

"Wilbur looks ridiculous," said Francine.

"Shhh!" said Hector. "He might hear you."

The curtain went up. The audience clapped. Morgan and Wilbur strutted into the spotlight on the stage.

"For my first trick," said Morgan, "I will remove eight knots from a piece of rope in one motion."

Wilbur handed him the rope. Morgan flipped an end into the air, and the knots disappeared.

The audience clapped. Morgan and Wilbur stepped forward and bowed. At that instant, Charles and Francine let the curtain drop. It fell on Morgan and Wilbur, burying them in folds of cloth.

"Help, help!" shouted Morgan as the audience booed and hollered. "You've jinxed my act, you dumb bunny!"

"No, I didn't," protested Wilbur. "It was an accident."

"We'll see about that," said Morgan, struggling to get free of the curtain.

The bunnies ran outside and hid behind a bush. "I have another idea," said Henrietta.

The others crowded close to hear . . .

The next afternoon, the four bunnies sneaked into the theater once again. Quietly they climbed to the platforms and ropes above the stage. They waited for the show to begin.

The curtain went up. Morgan and Wilbur pranced onstage dressed in robes and turbans. "I am Morgan the Magnificent!" said Morgan.

He pulled scarves out of his sleeves. He made a quarter disappear. "And now," he said, "I will saw my assistant in half."

Morgan wheeled a box onto the stage. Wilbur's knees shook as he climbed in. As Morgan lifted the saw, Wilbur closed his eyes.

The four bunnies formed a ladder, each one holding the other's legs. Francine was at the bottom. She grabbed Morgan's turban off his head.

The audience laughed and booed. Morgan's face grew as red as a radish. He reached for his turban, and it wasn't there. He got so mad, he smacked the box. The sides fell down, and there was Wilbur, scrunched into one end. The audience laughed and booed louder.

Quickly Morgan started to wheel Wilbur off the stage.

By this time, the bunnies were back in their hiding place. They lowered a big hook. It caught Morgan by the pants. The pants ripped, and the audience roared.

Morgan struggled to hide his underwear with his robe. He pushed Wilbur the rest of the way offstage. A moment later, he wheeled back a table with a huge top hat on it. "And now," he yelled desperately, "for my best trick, I will pull a very large rabbit out of a very large hat."

Morgan waved his wand and said *Abracadabra.* Suddenly eight furry paws yanked the cloth off the table. There lay Wilbur, trembling underneath.

The audience laughed and booed and booed. They threw rotten eggs and tomatoes.

"Wilbur, you've brought me nothing but trouble!" said Morgan. "You're fired!"

Shaking and quaking, Wilbur ran out of the theater. He ran and ran and ran and ran. He ran so far so fast, he was home before he knew it.

The piles of Easter eggs and jelly beans and chocolate candy had never looked so wonderful.

By the time Hector, Francine, Charles, and Henrietta reached Wilbur's house, he was relaxing in his favorite chair and adding the final touches to a few more Easter eggs.

"We're sorry we ruined your magic act," said Hector.

"We had to bring you back," said Francine.

"Well, you certainly messed things up," said Wilbur.

He finished painting the last egg and put it in a basket. "But you know something?" he added. "I'm really glad to be home."

"Hooray!" shouted the four bunnies. They hugged Wilbur.

He smiled. "I'm looking forward to delivering these eggs," he said.

And on Easter morning, before the sun rose, that's exactly what he did.